Published in the United States by Grolier Books, a division of Grolier Enterprises, Inc.

First American Edition.

ISBN: 0-7172-8473-5

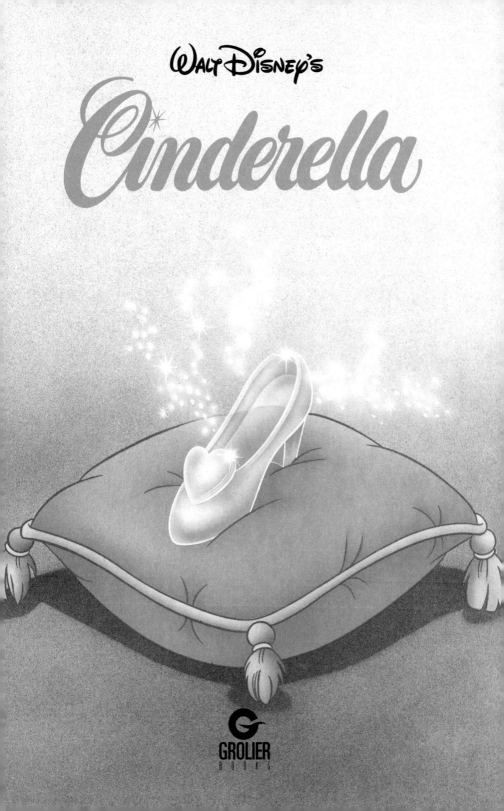

Once upon a time there was a beautiful girl named Cinderella. She was so kind that even the mice and the birds were her friends.

Each morning the birds woke her from her sweet dreams with their song.

Cinderella lived with her cruel stepmother and her two stepsisters, Anastasia and Drizella. They treated her like a servant.

Cinderella had to do all the cooking and sewing and washing and scrubbing.

Her stepsisters never did any work.

One day a royal messenger came
to the house.

He brought a letter from the King!

The Stepmother read
the letter.

The King was giving a
Royal Ball for the Prince
that night. Every girl in
the kingdom was invited.

"That means I can go!"
Cinderella cried.

Her stepsisters laughed.

"Imagine, Cinderella
dancing with the Prince!"
Drizella cackled.

"She's only fit to
dance with a broom,"
added Anastasia.

"But the letter says
every girl is invited,"
Cinderella insisted.

"So it does," the Stepmother agreed. "You may go—*if* you get all your work done. And *if* you can find something to wear."

"Oh, thank you!" said Cinderella. She quickly ran up to her room.

Cinderella pulled a
dress out of her trunk.

"This was my mother's
dress," she told the mice.
"Isn't it lovely? It just
needs some decoration."

Cinderella's mice had
never seen her so happy.

A thin mouse named
Jaq thought Cinderella
would be the prettiest girl
at the ball. A fat mouse
named Gus agreed.

Cinderella took out her sewing basket.
"I'll need a sash and some beads," she said.

Just then her stepmother shouted, "Cinderella!"

Cinderella hurried downstairs.

"Cinderella, wash the floors," her stepmother ordered.

"But I washed them yesterday," Cinderella said.

"Well, wash them again!" snapped the cruel woman. "And dust the drapes and clean the windows and finish the sewing."

The mice felt sorry for Cinderella.

"Cinderelly, do this! Cinderelly, do that!"
Jaq said. "Cinderelly will never have time to
fix her dress. Then her stepmother won't have
to let her go to the ball."

"Poor Cinderelly," Gus agreed.

One of the mice had an idea. "Why don't we fix the dress for Cinderelly? We can do it!"

All the animals agreed to help. Gus and Jaq sneaked into the stepsisters' room. Drizella and Anastasia were getting ready for the ball.

"This sash is old," Anastasia said. "These beads are horrible," Drizella said. They threw their things away.

Gus and Jaq took the sash and the beads.

"Pretty, pretty!" Gus exclaimed.

"Shh!" Jaq hissed. He was afraid they would wake Lucifer, the cat.

But the mice made it safely back to the attic.

Soon every beak
and paw was busy.

The animals measured . . .
. . . and cut . . .
. . . and sewed.
While they worked . . .

. . . Cinderella helped
her stepsisters with
their gowns.

Soon it was time to
leave for the ball.
"Why, Cinderella,"
her stepmother sneered.
"You're not ready.
What a shame."

Cinderella slowly climbed the stairs to her room.

"Oh, well, what's a Royal Ball," she said. "It would probably be dull and boring and . . ." Cinderella sighed. "Completely wonderful!"

But her dress wasn't finished. She couldn't go.

Cinderella opened the door to her room.

"Surprise!" shouted the mice and birds.

Cinderella thought she was dreaming. Her dress was beautiful!

"Oh, thank you!" Cinderella told her little friends.

She put on the gown and hurried downstairs.

"Isn't my dress lovely? May I go to the ball?" Cinderella asked.

Anastasia and Drizella gasped.

"Mother, she can't!"

"Well, we did have a bargain," began the Stepmother.

At that moment the sisters recognized the things they'd thrown away.

"My sash!" Anastasia wailed.

"My beads!" Drizella shrieked.

The sisters tore at Cinderella's gown. They took back the sash and the beads. Cinderella was left in rags.

Then Drizella and Anastasia went to the ball with their mother.

Cinderella ran into the
garden. She tried to
remember her sweet
dreams. But she didn't
think they would ever
come true!

Her animal friends
had never seen her so sad.

"There's nothing left to believe in. Nothing!"
Cinderella sobbed.

She didn't notice the lights that twinkled
and danced all around her.

But Jaq and Gus did. They could hardly
believe their eyes. The lights turned into
a kind-looking woman!

The woman patted
Cinderella's head.
She said, "You must
believe in something,
or I couldn't be here . . .

. . . and here I am! So dry
your tears. Now where
did I put my wand?"
    The woman was
Cinderella's fairy
godmother!

Everything she needed
to help Cinderella was
right in the garden.

The Fairy Godmother waved her wand.
Bibbidi, bobbidi, boo!
Four mice became four white horses.

Bibbidi, bobbidi, boo!

A pumpkin turned into a beautiful coach.

A horse became the coachman, and a dog became the footman.

The Fairy Godmother was very pleased.

"Hop in, my dear. We can't waste time," she urged.

"Don't you think my dress," Cinderella began.

"Good heavens, child! You can't go like *that*," said the Fairy Godmother.

Bibbidi, bobbidi, boo!

Suddenly Cinderella was wearing the gown of her dreams. And on her feet she wore glass slippers.

The Fairy Godmother said, "Like all dreams, my magic must end. At midnight the spell will be broken."

Cinderella promised to be home
before midnight. Off she rode to the ball!

The ball had already begun.
The King was not very happy.

He wanted his son to marry. The Prince had danced
with all the girls at the ball. But he had not fallen in
love with any of them.

"Love at first sight only happens in fairy tales," the
Duke told the King.

At that moment Cinderella made her entrance.
The Prince stared in wonder.
Here was the girl of his dreams!
The Prince asked Cinderella to dance.

Cinderella and the Prince danced
around the ballroom.

Everyone wondered about the beautiful girl.
"Do we know her?" Drizella asked.
"The Prince seems to," Anastasia said jealously.
"There is something familiar about her," the
Stepmother said.

When the dance ended,
Cinderella and the Prince
walked in the garden.

They were falling in love.
Suddenly the clock began to
strike midnight!
"I must go!" cried Cinderella.

"Wait!" called the Prince. But Cinderella couldn't wait.

As she fled, she lost one of her glass slippers.

The Prince showed
the glass slipper to
the Duke.

"Find the girl whose
foot fits this slipper.
I will marry her!" the
Prince said.

Meanwhile Cinderella's dress had become rags
again. The coach was now a pumpkin. The horses had
become mice again. And the coachman and footman
had turned back into a horse and a dog.

All Cinderella had left was one glass slipper.

The Duke searched
the entire kingdom
for the girl whose foot
fit the slipper. Soon
everyone knew that
the Prince would
marry that girl.

When Cinderella heard this, she got a dreamy look
in her eyes. The Stepmother saw the dreamy look.

She didn't want Cinderella to marry the Prince.

So she locked
Cinderella in
her room!
The Stepmother
put the key in her
pocket and left.
Gus and Jaq
saw everything.

"We've gotta get that key!"
Jaq cried. Gus agreed.
The two brave mice
managed to get the key from
the Stepmother's pocket.

They struggled
to get the big,
heavy key up the
tall stairs.

Jaq and Gus had to hurry! The Duke had just
arrived. His footman carried the glass slipper.

Anastasia tried on the slipper. Her foot was much too big!

Drizella tried next. She couldn't even fit her toes into the slipper!

"Are there any other ladies in the house?" asked the Duke.

"There is no one else," the Stepmother answered.

The Duke was about to leave when . . .

. . . Cinderella came down the stairs! Jaq and Gus had freed her!

"May I try on the slipper?" she asked.

But the cruel stepmother tripped the footman. The footman fell. And the slipper broke!

Luckily Cinderella had the other glass slipper. Of course, it fit perfectly!

Cinderella and the Prince were
soon married.

It was Cinderella's dream
come true.

Jaq and Gus weren't surprised
because they always knew that if you
keep on believing, that's just what
dreams do!